Jennifer Maher

The Happy Half-Moon Girl

Bumblebee Books
London

BUMBLEBEE PAPERBACK EDITION

Copyright © Jennifer Maher 2021

The right of Jennifer Maher to be identified as author and illustrator of
this work has been asserted in accordance with sections 77 and 78 of the Copyright, Designs and Patents Act 1988.

A CIP catalogue record for this title is
available from the British Library.

ISBN: 978-1-83934-299-8

Bumblebee Books is an imprint of
Olympia Publishers.

First Published in 2021

Bumblebee Books
Tallis House
2 Tallis Street
London
EC4Y 0AB

Printed in Great Britain

www.olympiapublishers.com

Dedication

For Casey and Cole.
Wishing you many nights of bedtime stories and sweet dreams.

On nights when
the moon is
big and bright

All little
children are
out of sight.

The moon is shining like a giant pearl

Hiding the happy half-moon girl.

When the moon is
covered half in shade

And the gleaming
glow begins to fade.

The half-moon girl raises her head

To smile down on the children asleep in their bed.

She gets into her moon clothes and lifts up her hand

Takes a deep breath and
blows into her dream wand.

She sends happy thoughts in a glimmering stream

To fill children's heads
with a joyful dream.

Dreams of unicorns, rainbows and sweets,

Of chocolate and ice-cream your favourite treats.

Dreams of mermaids under the sea

Or being so small you can ride on a bee.

Dreams of the circus and learning to fly,

Bouncing on clouds high up in the sky.

Dreams of fairies that fit
in your pocket

Or blasting off in your very own rocket.

So when you wake up smiling and all in a whirl

Remember, be thankful to the happy half-moon girl.

SWEET DREAMS

About the Author

Jennifer always had a love for all things creative and started writing poetry at a young age. A talent for drawing led her to college to study computer animation followed by courses on digital and freehand illustration. From this Jennifer discovered her true passion lay in storytelling and illustration. Bringing to life the story of *The Happy Half-Moon Girl*. Jennifer lives in Ireland, Co Meath with her husband, Derek, her daughter, Casey, and son, Cole.

Printed in Great Britain
by Amazon